Poems for the Young

Poems for the Young

Selected by Neil Philip
Illustrated by John Lawrence

STEWART, TABORI & CHANG
NEW YORK

Published in 1992 by Stewart, Tabori & Chang, Inc.
575 Broadway
New York, NY 10012

An Albion Book

Designer: Emma Bradford
Copy-editor: Robyn Marsack
Project co-ordinator: Elizabeth Wilkes

Library of Congress Cataloging-in-Publication Data

Poems for the young/selected by Neil Philip: illustrated by John Lawrence.
p. cm.
Summary: An illustrated collection of traditional rhymes and
modern poems on a variety of subjects.
ISBN 1–55670–262–0
1. Children's poetry, English. 2. Children's poetry, American.
[1. English poetry — Collections. 2. American poetry — Collections.]
I. Philip , Neil. II. Lawrence, John, 1933 – ill. III. Title.
PR1175.3.P57 1992
821.008' 09282—dc20   92–344
                                                                          CIP
                                                                          AC

Distributed in the U.S. by Workman Publishing
708 Broadway, New York, NY 10003

Distributed in Canada by Canadian Manda Group
P.O. Box 920, Station U, Toronto, Ontario M8Z 5P9

Typesetting and color origination by York House, London
Printed and bound in Hong Kong by South China Printing Co.

10 9 8 7 6 5 4 3 2 1

First edition

CONTENTS

THE PASTURE

I'm going out to clean the pasture spring;
I'll only stop to rake the leaves away
(And wait to watch the water clear, I may):
I sha'n't be gone long. – You come too.

I'm going out to fetch the little calf
That's standing by the mother. It's so young
It totters when she licks it with her tongue.
I sha'n't be gone long. – You come too.

ROBERT FROST

"ADAM AND EVE AND PINCHME"

Adam and Eve and Pinchme
Went down to the river to bathe.
Adam and Eve were drowned –
Who do you think was saved?

TRADITIONAL

THREE LITTLE GIRLS

Three little girls were sitting on a rail,
    Sitting on a rail,
    Sitting on a rail;
Three little girls were sitting on a rail,
  On a fine hot day in September.

What did they talk about that fine day,
    That fine day,
    That fine day?
What did they talk about that fine day,
  That fine hot day in September?

The crows and the corn they talked about,
    Talked about,
    Talked about;
But nobody knows what was said by the crows,
  On that fine hot day in September.

KATE GREENAWAY

ONE, TWO, BUCKLE MY SHOE

One, two,
Buckle my shoe;
Three, four,
Shut the door;
Five, six,
Pick up sticks;
Seven, eight,
Lay them straight;
Nine, ten,
A big fat hen;
Eleven, twelve,
Who will delve?
Thirteen, fourteen,
Maids a-courting;
Fifteen, sixteen,
Maids a-kissing;
Seventeen, eighteen,
Maids a-waiting;
Nineteen, twenty,
My stomach's empty.

TRADITIONAL

THE OLD GREY GOOSE

Go and tell Aunt Nancy,
Go and tell Aunt Nancy,
Go and tell Aunt Nancy,
  The old grey goose is dead.

The one that she was saving,
The one that she was saving,
The one that she was saving,
  To make a feather bed.

She died on Friday,
She died on Friday,
She died on Friday,
  Behind the old barn shed.

She left nine goslings,
She left nine goslings,
She left nine goslings,
  To scratch for their own bread.

TRADITIONAL

HIGGLETY, PIGGLETY, POP!

Higglety, pigglety, pop!
The dog has eaten the mop;
The pig's in a hurry,
The cat's in a flurry,
Higglety, pigglety, pop!

SAMUEL GRISWOLD GOODRICH

15

LADY MOON

O Lady Moon, your horns point toward the east;
    Shine, be increased:
O Lady Moon, your horns point toward the west;
    Wane, be at rest.

CHRISTINA ROSSETTI

GIRLS AND BOYS COME
OUT TO PLAY

Girls and boys come out to play,
The moon doth shine as bright as day!

    Leave your supper and leave your sleep,
    Come with your playfellows into the street.

Come with a whistle, come with a call,
Come with a good will or come not at all.

    Up the ladder and down the wall,
    A halfpenny roll will serve us all.

You find milk and I'll find flour,
And we'll have a pudding in half an hour.

TRADITIONAL

MINNIE AND MATTIE

Minnie and Mattie
   And fat little May,
Out in the country,
   Spending a day.

Such a bright day,
   With the sun glowing,
And the trees half in leaf,
   And the grass growing.

Pinky white pigling
   Squeals through his snout,
Woolly white lambkin
   Frisks all about.

Cluck! cluck! the nursing hen
   Summons her folk,–
Ducklings all downy soft,
   Yellow as yolk.

Cluck! cluck! the mother hen
   Summons her chickens
To peck the dainty bits
   Found in her pickings.

Minnie and Mattie
   And May carry posies,
Half of sweet violets,
   Half of primroses.

Give the sun time enough,
   Glowing and glowing,
He'll rouse the roses
   And bring them blowing.

Don't wait for roses
   Losing today,
O Minnie, Mattie,
   And wise little May.

Violets and primroses
   Blossom today
For Minnie and Mattie
   And fat little May.

CHRISTINA ROSSETTI

17

THE OLD MAN'S TOES

Up the street,
Down the street,
My
    Joan
        goes—
(Mind you don't tread upon the
Old
    Man's
        Toes!)
She hops along the pavement
Into every Square,
But she mustn't touch the Cracks in
  between
Them
    There.
The Squares on the pavement
Are safe
      as can
         be:
One is the Sands
By the side
      of the
         sea;
One is a Garden where
Joan's
    flowers
        grow;
One is a Meadow
She
   and I
      know.
But the Cracks are *dangerous,*
As
  Everybody
      knows!
The Cracks in the Pavement are the
  Old
    Man's
      Toes.

Any one who treads on the
Old
    Man's
      Corn
Will wish in a jiffy he had
Never
    been
      born!
For the Sea will roll up and
Suck
   you
     down!
And a horrid blight will turn your
Garden
    brown!
And into the Meadow with an
Angry
    Moo
A Big Cross Cow will come
Rushing
   at
     You!
Up the street and down the street
My
   Joan
      goes—
Here she makes a Pudding,
There she smells a Rose,
Yonder she goes stooping where the
Mushroom
      grows—
(Mind, Joan! don't tread upon the
Old
   Man's
     Toes!)

ELEANOR FARJEON

POEM

As the cat
climbed over
the top of

the jamcloset
first the right
forefoot

carefully
then the hind
stepped down

into the pit of
the empty
flowerpot

WILLIAM CARLOS WILLIAMS

UPON HER FEET

Her pretty feet
Like snails did creep
A little out, and then,
As if they started at bo-peep,
Did soon draw in again.

ROBERT HERRICK

POEM FOR NTOMBE IAYO
(AT FIVE WEEKS OF AGE)

who them people think
they are putting
me down here
on this floor

i'll just lay
here stretching
my arms and maybe i'll kick
my legs a li'l bit

why i betcha i'll just get up
from here and walk
soons i get big

NIKKI GIOVANNI

"MY BABY HAS A MOTTLED FIST"

My baby has a mottled fist,
  My baby has a neck in creases:
My baby kisses and is kissed,
  For he's the very thing for kisses.

CHRISTINA ROSSETTI

"HOW MANY DAYS HAS MY BABY TO PLAY?"

How many days has my baby to play?
Saturday, Sunday, Monday,
Tuesday, Wednesday, Thursday, Friday,
Saturday, Sunday, Monday.
Hop away, skip away,
My baby wants to play;
My baby wants to play every day.

TRADITIONAL

WHAT SOMEONE SAID WHEN HE WAS SPANKED ON THE DAY BEFORE HIS BIRTHDAY

Some day
I may
Pack my bag and run away.
Some day
I may.
—But not today.

Some night
I might
Slip away in the moonlight.
I might.
Some night.
—But not tonight.

Some night.
Some day.
I might.
I may.
—But right now I think I'll stay.

JOHN CIARDI

WHOLE DUTY OF CHILDREN

A child should always say what's true,
And speak when he is spoken to,
And behave mannerly at table:
At least as far as he is able.

ROBERT LOUIS STEVENSON

HAPPINESS

John had
Great Big
Waterproof
Boots on;
John had a
Great Big
Waterproof
Hat;

John had a
Great Big
Waterproof
Mackintosh –
And that
(Said John)
Is
That.

A. A. MILNE

"FAL DE RAL LA, FAL DE RAL LA"

Fal de ral la, fal de ral la,
Hinkumbooby round about.
Right hands in and left hands out,
Hinkumbooby round about;
Fal de ral la, fal de ral la,
Hinkumbooby round about.

Left hands in and right hands out,
Hinkumbooby round about;
Fal de ral la, fal de ral la,
Hinkumbooby round about.

Heads in and backs out,
Hinkumbooby round about;
Fal de ral la, &c.

Backs in and heads out,
Hinkumbooby round about;
Fal de ral la, &c.

A' feet in and nae feet out,
Hinkumbooby round about;
Fal de ral la, &c.

Right foot in and left foot out,
Hinkumbooby round about;
Fal de ral la, fal de ral la,
Hinkumbooby round about.

Left foot in and right foot out,
Hinkumbooby round about;
Fal de ral la, &c.

Shake hands a', shake hands a',
Hinkumbooby round about;
Fal de ral la, &c.

Good night a', good night a',
Hinkumbooby round about;
Fal de ral la, fal de ral la,
Hinkumbooby round about.

TRADITIONAL

SIMPLE GIFTS

'Tis the gift to be simple,
'Tis the gift to be free,
'Tis the gift to come down
Where we ought to be,
And when we find ourselves
In the place just right,
'Twill be in the valley
Of love and delight.
When true simplicity is gained,
To bow and to bend
We sha'n't be ashamed,
To turn, turn will be our delight,
Till by turning, turning
We come round right.

ANONYMOUS, SHAKER SONG

THERE'S A BLACK BOY IN A RING

There's a black boy in a ring, tra la la la la,
There's a black boy in a ring, tra la la la la,
There's a black boy in a ring, tra la la la la,
He like sugar an I like plum.

Wheel an take you pardner, jump shamador!
Wheel an take you pardner, jump shamador!
Wheel an take you pardner, jump shamador!
For he like sugar an I like plum.

TRADITIONAL

"TOM, HE WAS A PIPER'S SON"

Tom, he was a piper's son,
He learnt to play when he was young,
And all the tune that he could play
Was, Over the hills and far away,
Over the hills and a great way off,
The wind shall blow my topknot off.

Tom with his pipe made such a noise
That he pleased both the girls and boys,
And they all stopped to hear him play
Over the hills and far away,
Over the hills and a great way off,
The wind shall blow my topknot off.

TRADITIONAL

26

ROBIN THE BOBBIN

Robin the Bobbin, the big-bellied Ben,
He ate more meat than fourscore men;
He ate a cow, he ate a calf,
He ate a butcher and a half;
He ate a church, he ate a steeple,
He ate the priest and all the people!
   A cow and a calf,
   An ox and a half,
   A church and a steeple,
   And all the good people,
And yet he complain'd that his stomach wasn't full.

TRADITIONAL

27

WINTER MOON

How thin and sharp is the moon tonight!
How thin and sharp and ghostly white
Is the slim curved crook of the moon tonight!

LANGSTON HUGHES

AMULET

Inside the Wolf's fang, the mountain of heather.
Inside the mountain of heather, the Wolf's fur.
Inside the Wolf's fur, the ragged forest.
Inside the ragged forest, the Wolf's foot.
Inside the Wolf's foot, the stony horizon.
Inside the stony horizon, the Wolf's tongue.
Inside the Wolf's tongue, the Doe's tears.
Inside the Doe's tears, the frozen swamp.
Inside the frozen swamp, the Wolf's blood.
Inside the Wolf's blood, the snow wind.
Inside the snow wind, the Wolf's eye.
Inside the Wolf's eye, the North Star.
Inside the North Star, the Wolf's fang.

TED HUGHES

CHARM AGAINST WITCHES

Black luggie, lammer bead,
Rowan-tree, and red thread,
Put the witches to their speed.

TRADITIONAL

"HEY-HOW FOR HALLOWEEN"

Hey-How for Halloween!
Aa the witches tae be seen,
Some black, an some green,
Hey-how for Halloween!

TRADITIONAL

LAZY WITCH

Lazy witch,
What's wrong with you?
 Get up and stir your magic brew.
 Here's candlelight to chase the gloom.
 Jump up and mount your flying broom
 And muster up your charms and spells
 And wicked grins and piercing yells.
 It's Halloween! There's work to do!
Lazy witch,
What's wrong with you?

MYRA COHN LIVINGSTON

29

THE KLEPTOMANIAC

Beware the Kleptomaniac
Who knows not wrong from right
He'll wait until you turn your back
Then steal everything in sight:

The nose from a snowman
(Be it carrot or coal)

The stick from a blindman
From the beggar his bowl

The smoke from a chimney
The leaves from a tree

A kitten's miaow
(Pretty mean you'll agree)

He'll pinch a used teabag
From out of the pot

A field of potatoes
And scoff the whole lot

(Is baby still there,
Asleep in its cot?)

He'll rob the baton
From a conductor on stage

All the books from the library
Page by page

He'll snaffle your shadow
As you bask in the sun

Pilfer the currants
From out of your bun

He'll lift the wind
Right out of your sails

Hold your hand
And make off with your nails

When he's around
Things just disappear

F nnily eno gh I th nk
Th re's one ar und h re!

ROGER MCGOUGH

THE FAIRIES

Up the airy mountain,
　　Down the rushy glen,
We daren't go a-hunting
　　For fear of little men;
Wee folk, good folk,
　　Trooping all together;
Green jacket, red cap,
　　And white owl's feather!

Down along the rocky shore
　　Some make their home,
They live on crispy pancakes
　　Of yellow tide-foam;
Some in the reeds
　　Of the black mountain-lake,
With frogs for their watchdogs,
　　All night awake.

High on the hill-top
　　The old King sits;
He is now so old and grey
　　He's nigh lost his wits.
With a bridge of white mist
　　Columbkill he crosses,
On his stately journeys
　　From Slieveleague to Rosses;
Or going up with music
　　On cold starry nights,
To sup with the Queen
　　Of the gay Northern Lights.

They stole little Bridget
  For seven years long;
When she came down again
  Her friends were all gone.
They took her lightly back,
  Between the night and morrow,
They thought that she was fast asleep,
  But she was dead with sorrow.
They have kept her ever since
  Deep within the lake,
On a bed of flag-leaves,
  Watching till she wake.

By the craggy hillside,
  Through the mosses bare,
They have planted thorn trees
  For pleasure, here and there.
Is any man so daring
  As dig them up in spite,
He shall find their sharpest thorns
  In his bed at night.

Up the airy mountain,
  Down the rushy glen,
We daren't go a-hunting
  For fear of little men;
Wee folk, good folk,
  Trooping all together;
Green jacket, red cap,
  And white owl's feather!

WILLIAM ALLINGHAM

33

THE JUMBLIES

They went to sea in a Sieve, they did,
    In a Sieve they went to sea;
In spite of all their friends could say,
On a winter's morn, on a stormy day,
    In a Sieve they went to sea!
And when the Sieve turned round and round,
And everyone cried, "You'll all be drowned!"
They called aloud, "Our Sieve ain't big,
But we don't care a button, we don't care a fig!
    In a Sieve we'll go to sea."
        Far and few, far and few,
            Are the lands where the Jumblies live;
            Their heads are green, and their hands are blue,
                And they went to sea in a Sieve.

34

They sailed away in a Sieve, they did,
    In a Sieve they sailed so fast;
With only a beautiful pea-green veil
Tied with a riband by way of a sail
    To a small tobacco-pipe mast;
And everyone said, who saw them go,
"O won't they be soon upset, you know,
For the sky is dark, and the voyage is long,
And happen what may, it's extremely wrong,
    In a Sieve to sail so fast."
        Far and few, far and few,
            Are the lands where the Jumblies live;
            Their heads are green, and their hands are blue,
            And they went to sea in a Sieve.

The water it soon came in, it did,
    The water it soon came in;
So to keep them dry, they wrapped their feet
In a pinky paper, all folded neat,
    And they fastened it down with a pin.
And they passed the night in a crockery jar,
And each of them said, "How wise we are!
Though the sky be dark and the voyage be long
Yet we never can think we were rash or wrong,
    While round in our Sieve we spin!"
        Far and few, far and few,
            Are the lands where the Jumblies live;
            Their heads are green, and their hands are blue,
            And they went to sea in a Sieve.

And all night long they sailed away;
    And when the sun went down,
They whistled and warbled a moony song,
To the echoing sound of a coppery gong,
    In the shade of the mountains brown.
"O Timballo! How happy we are,
When we live in a Sieve and a crockery jar,
And all night long in the moonlight pale,
We sail away with a pea-green sail
    In the shade of the mountains brown!"
        Far and few, far and few,
            Are the lands where the Jumblies live;
            Their heads are green, and their hands are blue,
            And they went to sea in a Sieve.

They sailed to the Western Sea, they did,
    To a land all covered with trees,
And they bought an Owl and a useful Cart,
And a pound of Rice and a Cranberry Tart,
    And a hive of silvery Bees.
And they bought a Pig, and some green Jack-daws,
And a lovely Monkey with lollipop paws,
And forty bottles of Ring-Bo-Ree,
    And no end of Stilton Cheese.
        Far and few, far and few,
            Are the lands where the Jumblies live;
            Their heads are green, and their hands are blue,
            And they went to sea in a Sieve.

And in twenty years they all came back,
   In twenty years or more.
And everyone said, "How tall they've grown!
For they've been to the Lakes, and the Torrible Zone,
   And the hills of the Chankly Bore;"
And they drank their health and gave them a feast
Of dumplings made of beautiful yeast;
And everyone said, "If we only live,
We, too, will go to sea in a Sieve –
   To the hills of the Chankly Bore!"
     Far and few, far and few,
       Are the lands where the Jumblies live;
       Their heads are green, and their hands are blue,
         And they went to sea in a Sieve.

EDWARD LEAR

37

SING A SONG OF PEOPLE

Sing a song of people
   Walking fast or slow;
People in the city,
   Up and down they go.

People on the sidewalk,
People on the bus;
People passing, passing,
In back and front of us.
People on the subway
Underneath the ground;
People riding taxis
Round and round and round.

People with their hats on,
Going in the doors;
People with umbrellas
When it rains and pours.
People in tall buildings
And in stores below;
Riding elevators
Up and down they go.

People walking singly,
People in a crowd;
People saying nothing,
People talking loud.
People laughing, smiling,
Grumpy people too;
People who just hurry
And never look at you!

Sing a song of people
   Who like to come and go;
Sing of city people
   You see but never know!

LOIS LENSKI

SING A SONG OF SUBWAYS

Sing a song of subways,
Never see the sun;
Four-and-twenty people
In room for one.

When the doors are opened–
Everybody run.

EVE MERRIAM

40

FROM A RAILWAY CARRIAGE

Faster than fairies, faster than witches,
Bridges and houses, hedges and ditches;
And charging along like troops in a battle,
All through the meadows the horses and cattle:
All of the sights of the hill and the plain
Fly as thick as driving rain;
And ever again, in the wink of an eye,
Painted stations whistle by.

Here is a child who clambers and scrambles,
All by himself and gathering brambles;
Here is a tramp who stands and gazes;
And there is the green for stringing the daisies!
Here is a cart run away in the road
Lumping along with man and load;
And here is a mill and there is a river:
Each a glimpse and gone for ever!

ROBERT LOUIS STEVENSON

HAPPY THOUGHT

The world is so full
    of a number of things,
I'm sure we should all
    be as happy as kings.

ROBERT LOUIS STEVENSON

THE STAR

Twinkle, twinkle, little star,
How I wonder what you are!
Up above the world so high,
Like a diamond in the sky.

When the blazing sun is gone,
When he nothing shines upon,
Then you show your little light,
Twinkle, twinkle, all the night.

Then the traveller in the dark,
Thanks you for your tiny spark,
He could not see which way to go,
If you did not twinkle so.

In the dark blue sky you keep,
And often through my curtains peep,
For you never shut your eye,
Till the sun is in the sky.

As your bright and tiny spark,
Lights the traveller in the dark–
Though I know not what you are,
Twinkle, twinkle, little star.

JANE TAYLOR

METAMORPHOSIS

When water turns ice does it remember
one time it was water?
When ice turns back into water does it
remember it was ice?

CARL SANDBURG

SUN

The sun
Is a leaping fire
Too hot
To go near,

But it will still
Lie down
In warm yellow squares
On the floor

Like a flat
Quilt, where
The cat can curl
And purr.

VALERIE WORTH

"QUACK!" SAID THE BILLY-GOAT

"Quack!" said the billy-goat,
"Oink!" said the hen.
"Miaow!" said the little chick
Running in the pen.

"Hobble-gobble!" said the dog.
"Cluck!" said the sow.
"Tu-whit-tu-whoo!" the donkey said.
"Baa!" said the cow.

"Hee-haw!" the turkey cried.
The duck began to moo.
And all at once the sheep went
"Cock-a-doodle-doo!"

The owl coughed and cleared his throat
And he began to bleat.
"Bow-wow!" said the cock
Swimming in the leat.

"Cheep-cheep!" said the cat
As she began to fly.
"Farmer's been and laid an egg –
That's the reason why."

CHARLES CAUSLEY

I SAW A JOLLY HUNTER

I saw a jolly hunter
  With a jolly gun
Walking in the·country
  In the jolly sun.

In the jolly meadow
  Sat a jolly hare.
Saw the jolly hunter.
  Took jolly care.

Hunter jolly eager –
  Sight of jolly prey.
Forgot gun pointing
  Wrong jolly way.

Jolly hunter jolly head
  Over heels gone.
Jolly old safety-catch
  Not jolly on.

Bang went the jolly gun.
  Hunter jolly dead.
Jolly hare got clean away.
  Jolly good, I said.

CHARLES CAUSLEY

THREE JOLLY HUNTSMEN

Three jolly huntsmen,
I've heard people say,
Went hunting together
On St David's Day.

All day they hunted,
And nothing could they find,
But a ship a-sailing,
A-sailing with the wind.

One said it was a ship,
The other he said, Nay;
The third said it was a house,
With the chimney blown away.

And all the night they hunted,
And nothing could they find
But the moon a-gliding,
A-gliding with the wind.

One said it was the moon,
The other he said, Nay;
The third said it was a cheese,
And half of it cut away.

And all the day they hunted,
And nothing did they find
But a hedgehog in a bramble-bush,
And that they left behind.

The first said it was a hedgehog,
The second he said, Nay;
The third said it was a pin cushion,
And the pins stuck in wrong way.

And all the day they hunted,
And nothing could they find
But an owl in a holly-tree,
And that they left behind.

One said it was an owl,
The second he said, Nay;
The third said 'twas an old man,
And his beard was growing grey.

TRADITIONAL

And all the night they hunted,
And nothing could they find
But a hare in a turnip-field,
And that they left behind.

The first said it was a hare,
The second he said, Nay;
The third said it was a calf,
And the cow had run away.

A FARMYARD SONG

I had a cat and the cat pleased me,
I fed my cat by yonder tree;
    Cat goes fiddle-i-fee.

I had a hen and the hen pleased me,
I fed my hen by yonder tree;
    Hen goes chimmy-chuck, chimmy-
      chuck,
    Cat goes fiddle-i-fee.

I had a duck and the duck pleased me,
I fed my duck by yonder tree;
    Duck goes quack, quack,
    Hen goes chimmy-chuck, chimmy-
      chuck,
    Cat goes fiddle-i-fee.

I had a goose and the goose pleased me,
I fed my goose by yonder tree;
    Goose goes swishy, swashy,
    Duck goes quack, quack,
    Hen goes chimmy-chuck, chimmy-
      chuck,
    Cat goes fiddle-i-fee.

I had a sheep and the sheep pleased me,
I fed my sheep by yonder tree;
    Sheep goes baa, baa,
    Goose goes swishy, swashy,
    Duck goes quack, quack,
    Hen goes chimmy-chuck, chimmy-
      chuck,
    Cat goes fiddle-i-fee.

I had a pig and the pig pleased me,
I fed my pig by yonder tree;
    Pig goes griffy, gruffy,
    Sheep goes baa, baa,
    Goose goes swishy, swashy,
    Duck goes quack, quack,
    Hen goes chimmy-chuck, chimmy-
      chuck,
    Cat goes fiddle-i-fee.

I had a cow and the cow pleased me,
I fed my cow by yonder tree;
    Cow goes moo, moo,
    Pig goes griffy, gruffy,
    Sheep goes baa, baa,
    Goose goes swishy, swashy,
    Duck goes quack, quack,
    Hen goes chimmy-chuck, chimmy-
      chuck,
    Cat goes fiddle-i-fee.

I had a horse and the horse pleased me,
I fed my horse by yonder tree;
    Horse goes neigh, neigh,
    Cow goes moo, moo,
    Pig goes griffy, gruffy,
    Sheep goes baa, baa,
    Goose goes swishy, swashy,
    Duck goes quack, quack,
    Hen goes chimmy-chuck, chimmy-
      chuck,
    Cat goes fiddle-i-fee.

I had a dog and the dog pleased me,
I fed my dog by yonder tree;
 Dog goes bow-wow, bow-wow,
 Horse goes neigh, neigh,
 Cow goes moo, moo,
 Pig goes griffy, gruffy,
 Sheep goes baa, baa,
 Goose goes swishy, swashy,
 Duck goes quack, quack,
 Hen goes chimmy-chuck, chimmy-
  chuck,
 Cat goes fiddle-i-fee.

TRADITIONAL

FROG WENT A-COURTIN'

Mr Froggie went a-courtin' an' he did ride;
Sword and pistol by his side.

He went to Missus Mousie's hall,
Gave a loud knock and gave a loud call.
"Pray, Missus Mousie, air you within?"
"Yes, kind sir, I set an' spin."

He tuk Miss Mousie on his knee,
An' sez, "Miss Mousie, will ya marry me?"
Miss Mousie blushed an' hung her head,
"You'll have t'ask Uncle Rat," she said.

"Not without Uncle Rat's consent
Would I marry the Pres-i-dent."

Uncle Rat jumped up an' shuck his fat side,
To think his niece would be Bill Frog's bride.
Nex' day Uncle Rat went to town,
To git his niece a weddin' gown.

Whar shall the weddin' supper be?
'Way down yander in a holler tree.
First come in was a Bumble-bee,
Who danced a jig with Captain Flea.
Next come in was a Butterfly,
Sellin' butter very high.

An' when they all set down to sup,
A big gray goose come an' gobbled 'em all up.

An' this is the end of one, two, three,
The Rat an' the Mouse an' the little Froggie.

TRADITIONAL

EPIGRAM

Engraved on the Collar of a Dog which I Gave to His Royal Highness

I am his Highness' Dog at Kew:
Pray tell me, sir, whose dog are you?

ALEXANDER POPE

DOG

Asleep he wheezes at his ease.
He only wakes to scratch his fleas.

He hogs the fire, he bakes his head
As if it were a loaf of bread.

He's just a sack of snoring dog.
You can lug him like a log.

You can roll him with your foot.
He'll stay snoring where he's put.

Take him out for exercise
He'll roll in cowclap up to his eyes.

He will not race, he will not romp.
He saves his strength for gobble and chomp.

He'll work as hard as you could wish
Emptying the dinner dish.

Then flops flat, and digs down deep,
Like a miner, into sleep.

TED HUGHES

SELF-PITY

I never saw a wild thing
sorry for itself.
A small bird will drop frozen dead from a bough
without ever having felt sorry for itself.

D. H. LAWRENCE

MRS PECK-PIGEON

Mrs Peck-Pigeon
Is pecking for bread,
Bob-bob-bob
Goes her little round head.
Tame as a pussy-cat
In the street,
Step-step-step
Go her little red feet.
With her little red feet
And her little round head,
Mrs Peck-Pigeon
Goes pecking for bread.

ELEANOR FARJEON

"I SAW A SHIP A-SAILING"

I saw a ship a-sailing
    A-sailing on the sea;
And, oh! it was all laden
    With pretty things for thee!

There were comfits in the cabin,
    And apples in the hold;
The sails were made of silk,
    And the masts were made of gold:

The four-and-twenty sailors
    That stood between the decks,
Were four-and-twenty white mice,
    With chains about their necks.

The captain was a duck,
    With a packet on his back;
And when the ship began to move,
    The captain said, "Quack! quack!"

TRADITIONAL

THE MONTHS OF THE YEAR

January brings the snow;
Makes the toes and fingers glow.

February brings the rain,
Thaws the frozen ponds again.

March brings breezes loud and shrill,
Stirs the dancing daffodil.

April brings the primrose sweet,
Scatters daisies at our feet.

May brings flocks of pretty lambs,
Skipping by their fleecy dams.

June brings tulips, lilies, roses;
Fills the children's hands with posies.

Hot July brings cooling showers,
Stawberries and gilly-flowers.

August brings the sheaves of corn,
Then the Harvest home is borne.

Warm September brings the fruit,
Sportsmen then begin to shoot.

Fresh October brings the pheasant,
Then to gather nuts is pleasant.

Dull November brings the blast,
Then the leaves are falling fast.

Chill December brings the sleet,
Blazing fire and Christmas treat.

SARA COLERIDGE

A BOY'S SONG

Where the pools are bright and deep,
Where the grey trout lies asleep,
Up the river and over the lea,
That's the way for Billy and me.

Where the blackbird sings the latest,
Where the hawthorn blooms the sweetest,
Where the nestlings chirp and flee,
That's the way for Billy and me.

Where the mowers mow the cleanest,
Where the hay lies thick and greenest,
There to track the homeward bee,
That's the way for Billy and me.

JAMES HOGG

DUCKS' DITTY

All along the backwater,
Through the rushes tall,
Ducks are a-dabbling.
Up tails all!

Ducks' tails, drakes' tails,
Yellow feet a-quiver,
Yellow bills all out of sight
Busy in the river!

Slushy green undergrowth
Where the roach swim—
Here we keep our larder,
Cool and full and dim.

Every one for what he likes!
We like to be
Heads down, tails up,
Dabbling free!

High in the blue above
Swifts whirl and call—
We are down a-dabbling
Up tails all!

KENNETH GRAHAME

THE COW

The friendly cow, all red and white,
I love with all my heart:
She gives me cream with all her might,
To eat with apple-tart.

She wanders lowing here and there,
And yet she cannot stray,
All in the pleasant open air,
The pleasant light of day;

And blown by all the winds that pass
And wet with all the showers,
She walks among the meadow grass
And eats the meadow flowers.

ROBERT LOUIS STEVENSON

HECTOR PROTECTOR

Hector Protector was dressed all in green;
Hector Protector was sent to the Queen.
The Queen did not like him,
Nor more did the King:
So Hector Protector was sent back again.

TRADITIONAL

THE COMPUTER'S FIRST CHRISTMAS CARD

jollymerry
hollyberry
jollyberry
merryholly
happyjolly
jollyjelly
jellybelly
bellymerry
hollyheppy
jollyMolly
merryJerry
merryHarry
hoppyBarry
heppyJarry
boppyheppy
berryjorry
jorryjolly
moppyjelly

Mollymerry
Jerryjolly
bellyboppy
jorryhoppy
hollymoppy
Barrymerry
Jarryheppy
happyboppy
boppyjolly
jollymerry
merrymerry
merrymerry
merryChris
ammerryasa
Chrismerry
asMERRYCHR
YSANTHEMUM

EDWIN MORGAN

ADVICE TO A CHILD

Set your fir-tree   Hang your stocking
In a pot;   By the fire,
Needles green   Empty of
Is all it's got.   Your heart's desire;
Shut the door   Up the chimney
And go away,   Say your say,
And so to sleep   And so to sleep
Till Christmas Day.   Till Christmas Day.
In the morning   In the morning
Seek your tree,   Draw the blind,
And you shall see   And you shall find
What you shall see.   What you shall find.

ELEANOR FARJEON

SNOW

I've just woken up and I'm lying in bed
With the end of a dream going round in my head,
And something much quieter and softer than rain
Is brushing the window pane.

It's snowing! It's snowing! My room's filled with light.
Outside it's like Switzerland, everything's white.
That bulge is our dustbin, that hummock's the wall.
I can't see the flower-beds at all.

I've got to get out there. I've got to get dressed.
I can't find my pants and I can't find my vest.
Who's taken my jumper? Who's hidden my belt?
It might be beginning to melt!

I'm outside. I'm running. I'm up to my waist.
I'm rolling. I'm tasting the metally taste.
There's snow down my trousers and snow up my nose.
I can't even feel my toes.

I'm tracking a polar bear over the ice,
I'm making a snow-man, he's fallen down twice,
I'm cutting some steps to the top of the hedge,
Tomorrow I'm building a sledge.

I'm lying in bed again, tucked up tight;
I know I'll sleep soundly and safely tonight.
My snow-man's on guard and his shiny black eyes
Are keeping a look-out for spies.

Sleep quietly, sleep deeply, sleep calmly, sleep curled
In warm woolly blankets while out in the world,
On field and forest and mountain and town
The snow flakes like feathers float down.

RICHARD EDWARDS

"GO TO BED FIRST"

Go to bed first,
A golden purse,
Go to bed second,
A golden bezant.
Go to bed third
A golden bird.

TRADITIONAL

"MY GRANDMOTHER SENT ME . . ."

My grandmother sent me a new-fashioned three cornered cambric country cut handkerchief. Not an old-fashioned three cornered cambric country cut handkerchief, but a new-fashioned three cornered cambric country cut handkerchief.

TRADITIONAL

"POOR MARY IS WEEPING"

Poor Mary is weeping, is weeping, is weeping,
Poor Mary is weeping on a bright summer's day.

Pray tell me what you're weeping for, weeping for,
  weeping for,
Pray tell me what you're weeping for, on a bright
  summer's day?

I'm weeping for my true love, my true love, my true love,
I'm weeping for my true love, on a bright summer's day.

Stand up and choose your lover, your lover, your lover,
Stand up and choose your lover, on a bright summer's day.

Go to church with your lover, your lover, your lover,
Go to church with your lover, on a bright summer's day.

Be happy in a ring, love; a ring, love; a ring, love.
Kiss both together, love, on this bright summer's day.

TRADITIONAL

65

THE GREAT PANJANDRUM

So she went into the garden
to cut a cabbage-leaf
to make an apple-pie;
and at the same time
a great she-bear, coming down the street,
pops its head into the shop.
What! no soap?
       So he died,
and she very imprudently married the Barber:
and there were present
the Piclillies,
       and the Joblillies,
           And the Garyulies,
and the great Panjandrum himself,
with the little round button at top;
and they all fell to playing the game of catch-as-catch-can,
till the gunpowder ran out at the heels of their boots.

SAMUEL FOOTE

STONE IN THE WATER

Stone in the water,
Stone on the sand,
Whom shall I marry
When I get to land?

Will he be handsome
Or will he be plain,
Strong as the sun
Or rich as the rain?

Will he be dark
Or will he be fair,
And what will be the colour
That shines in his hair?

Will he come late
Or will he come soon,
At morning or midnight
Or afternoon?

What will he say
Or what will he sing,
And will he be holding
A plain gold ring?

Stone in the water
Still and small,
Tell me if he comes,
Or comes not at all.

CHARLES CAUSLEY

BOO TO A GOOSE

"I wouldn't say Boo
To a goose
If I were you"
Says Boo

Who

Has said it once too
Often now
And finds the goose is
Tired of his excuses

Ow!

BOO HOO

JOHN MOLE

DON'T CALL ALLIGATOR LONG-
MOUTH TILL YOU CROSS RIVER

Call alligator long-mouth
call alligator saw-mouth
call alligator pushy-mouth
call alligator scissors-mouth
call alligator raggedy-mouth
call alligator bumpy-bum
call alligator all dem rude word
but better wait
                    till you cross river.

JOHN AGARD

THE DUEL

The gingham dog and the calico cat
    Side by side on the table sat;
'Twas half-past twelve, and (what do you think!)
Nor one nor t'other had slept a wink!
    The old Dutch clock and the Chinese plate
    Appeared to know as sure as fate
There was going to be a terrible spat.
    (I wasn't there; I simply state
    What was told to me by the Chinese plate!)

The gingham dog went "bow-wow-wow!"
And the calico cat replied "mee-ow!"
The air was littered, an hour or so,
With bits of gingham and calico,
    While the old Dutch clock in the
        chimney-place
    Up with its hands before its face,
For it always dreaded a family row!
    (Now mind: I'm only telling you
    What the old Dutch clock declares is true!)

The Chinese plate looked very blue,
And wailed, "Oh, dear! what shall we do?"
But the gingham dog and the calico cat
Wallowed this way and tumbled that,
    Employing every tooth and claw
    In the awfullest way you ever saw—
And, oh! how the gingham and calico flew!
    (Don't fancy I exaggerate!
    I got my news from the Chinese plate!)

Next morning, where the two had sat,
They found no trace of dog or cat;
And some folks think unto this day
That burglars stole that pair away!
    But the truth about the cat and pup
    Is this: they ate each other up!
Now what do you really think of that!
    (The old Dutch clock it told me so,
    And that is how I came to know.)

EUGENE FIELD

73

SOURWOOD MOUNTAIN

Chickens a-crowin' on Sourwood Mountain,
  Ho-dee-ing-dong-doodle allay day,
So many pretty girls I can't count 'em,
  Ho-dee-ing-dong-doodle allay day.

My true love, she's a blue-eyed dandy,
  Ho-dee-ing-dong-doodle allay day,
A kiss from her is sweeter than candy,
  Ho-dee-ing-dong-doodle allay day.

My true love lives over the river,
  Ho-dee-ing-dong-doodle allay day,
A hop and a skip and I'll be with her,
  Ho-dee-ing-dong-doodle allay day.

My true love is a blue-eyed daisy,
  Ho-dee-ing-dong-doodle allay day,
If she don't marry me I'll go crazy,
  Ho-dee-ing-dong-doodle allay day.

Back my jenny up the Sourwood Mountain.
  Ho-dee-ing-dong-doodle allay day,
So many pretty girls I can't count 'em,
  Ho-dee-ing-dong-doodle allay day.

My true love is a sunburnt daisy,
  Ho-dee-ing-dong-doodle allay day,
She won't work and I'm too lazy,
  Ho-dee-ing-dong-doodle allay day.

TRADITIONAL

THERE WAS A LITTLE GIRL

There was a little girl
Who had a little curl
Right in the middle of her forehead.
When she was good
She was very, very good,
But when she was bad she was horrid.

HENRY WADSWORTH LONGFELLOW

from THE PEOPLE, YES

"Why did the children
put beans in their ears
when the one thing we told the children
they must not do
was put beans in their ears?"

"Why did the children
pour molasses on the cat
when the one thing we told the children
they must not do
was pour molasses on the cat?"

CARL SANDBURG

PEAS

I always eat peas with honey,
I've done it all my life,
They do taste kind of funny
But it keeps them on the knife.

ANONYMOUS

"PEASE-PORRIDGE HOT"

Pease-porridge hot,
  Pease-porridge cold,
Pease-porridge in the pot,
  Nine days old.

Some like it hot,
  Some like it cold,
Some like it in the pot
  Nine days old.

TRADITIONAL

ME, MYSELF, AND I

Me, myself, and I –
We went to the kitchen and ate a pie.
Then my mother she came in
And chased us out with a rolling pin.

ANONYMOUS

HOW MANY MILES TO BABYLON?

How many miles to Babylon?
Threescore and ten, Sir.

Can I get there by candlelight?
Oh yes, and back again, Sir.

If your heels are nimble and light,
You may get there by candlelight.

TRADITIONAL

WIND-FLOWERS

"Twist me a crown of wind-flowers;
    That I may fly away
To hear the singers at their song,
    And players at their play."

"Put on your crown of wind-flowers:
    But whither would you go?"
"Beyond the surging of the sea
    And the storms that blow."

"Alas! your crown of wind-flowers
    Can never make you fly:
I twist them in a crown today,
    And tonight they die."

CHRISTINA ROSSETTI

I MET A MAN

As I was going up the stair
I met a man who wasn't there.
He wasn't there again today –
Oh! how I wish he'd go away!

ANONYMOUS

79

OLD SHELLOVER

"Come!" said Old Shellover.
"What?" says Creep.
"The horny old Gardener's fast asleep;
The fat cock Thrush
To his nest has gone;
And the dew shines bright
In the rising Moon;
Old Sallie Worm from her hole doth peep:
Come!" said Old Shellover.
"Ay!" said Creep.

WALTER DE LA MARE

SMALL, SMALLER

I thought that I knew all there was to know
Of being small, until I saw once, black against the snow,
A shrew, trapped in my footprint, jump and fall
And jump again and fall, the hole too deep, the walls too tall.

RUSSELL HOBAN

THE MOUSE'S LULLABY

Oh, rock-a-by, baby mouse, rock-a-by, so!
When baby's asleep to the baker's I'll go,
And while he's not looking I'll pop from a hole,
And bring to my baby a fresh penny roll.

PALMER COX

THE WHITE SEAL'S LULLABY

Oh! hush thee, my baby, the night is behind us,
    And black are the waters that sparkled so green.
The moon, o'er the combers, looks downward to find us
    At rest in the hollows that rustle between.

Where billow meets billow, there soft be thy pillow;
    Ah, weary wee flipperling, curl at thy ease!
The storm shall not wake thee, nor shark overtake thee,
    Asleep in the arms of the slow-swinging seas.

RUDYARD KIPLING

FOG

The fog comes
on little cat feet.
It sits looking
over harbour and city
on silent haunches
and then moves on.

CARL SANDBURG

SWEET AND LOW

Sweet and low, sweet and low,
  Wind of the western sea,
Low, low, breathe and blow,
  Wind of the western sea!
  Over the rolling waters go,
  Come from the dying moon, and blow,
  Blow him again to me;
While my little one, while my pretty one sleeps.

Sleep and rest, sleep and rest,
  Father will come to thee soon;
Rest, rest, on mother's breast,
  Father will come to thee soon;
  Father will come to his babe in the nest,
  Silver sails all out of the west
  Under the silver moon;
Sleep, my little one, sleep, my pretty one, sleep.

ALFRED, LORD TENNYSON

DREAMS

Here we are all, by day; by night we are hurled
By dreams, each one into a several world.

ROBERT HERRICK

W

The King sent for his wise men all
   To find a rhyme for W;
When they had thought a good long time
But could not think of a single rhyme,
   "I'm sorry," said he, "to trouble you."

JAMES REEVES

A GIRL

The tree has entered my hands,
The sap has ascended my arms,
The tree has grown in my breast—
Downward,
The branches grow out of me, like arms.

Tree you are,
Moss you are,
You are violets with wind above them.
A child – *so high* – you are,
And all this is folly to the world.

EZRA POUND

TUMBLING

In jumping and tumbling
    We spend the whole day,
Till night by arriving
    Has finished our play.

What then? One and all,
    There's no more to be said,
As we tumbled all day,
    So we tumble to bed.

ANONYMOUS

A CRADLE SONG

Golden slumbers kiss your eyes,
Smiles awake you when you rise.
Sleep, pretty wantons, do not cry,
And I will sing a lullaby:
Rock them, rock them, lullaby.

Care is heavy, therefore sleep you;
You are care, and care must keep you.
Sleep, pretty wantons, do not cry,
And I will sing a lullaby:
Rock them, rock them, lullaby.

THOMAS DEKKER

86

"LIE A-BED"

Lie a-bed,
Sleepy head,
Shut up eyes, bo-peep;
Till day-break
Never wake:–
Baby, sleep.

CHRISTINA ROSSETTI

INDEX OF TITLES AND FIRST LINES

Titles are in *italics*. Where the title and the first line are the same, the first line only is listed.

INDEX OF POETS

ACKNOWLEDGMENTS

We would like to thank all the authors, publishers and literary representatives, who have given permission to reprint poems in this collection.

John Agard: to Caroline Sheldon Literary Agency on behalf of the author for 'Don't Call Alligator Long-Mouth Till You Cross River' from SAY IT AGAIN GRANNY (Bodley Head, 1986); Charles Causley: to David Higham Associates Ltd for 'I Saw a Jolly Hunter' from COLLECTED POEMS (Macmillan), ' "Quack!" said the Billy-goat' from FIGGIE HOBBIN (Macmillan) and 'Stone in the Water' from EARLY IN THE MORNING (Viking Kestrel, 1986); John Ciardi: to Judith Ciardi for 'What Someone Said When He Was Spanked on the Day Before His Birthday' from YOU KNOW WHO (Harper & Row, 1964); Walter de la Mare: to The Literary Trustees of Walter de la Mare and The Society of Authors as their representative for 'Old Shellover' from COLLECTED RHYMES AND VERSES (Faber & Faber, 1970); Richard Edwards: to Lutterworth Press, PO. Box 60, Cambridge for 'Snow' from THE WORD PARTY (Lutterworth Press, 1986); Eleanor Farjeon: to David Higham Associates Ltd. for 'The Old Man's Toes', 'Mrs Peck Pigeon' and 'Advice to a child' from THE CHILDRENS BELLS (Oxford University Press) and SILVER SAND AND SNOW (Michael Joseph Ltd); Robert Frost: to Henry Holt & Co. Inc. for 'The Pasture' from ROBERT FROST: SELECTED BY HIMSELF (Penguin Poets, 1955); Nikki Giovanni: to Farrar, Straus & Giroux Inc. for 'Poem for Ntombe Iayo (at five weeks of age)' from SPIN A SOFT BLACK SONG (1985). Copyright © by 1971 Nikki Giovanni; Russell Hoban: to David Higham Associates Ltd for 'Small, Smaller' from THE PEDALLING MAN (Heinemann); Langston Hughes: to Alfred A. Knopf Inc. for 'Winter Moon' from SELECTED POEMS. Copyright 1926 by Alfred A. Knopf Inc. and renewed 1954 by Langston Hughes; Ted Hughes: to Faber & Faber Ltd and Viking Penguin Inc. for 'Amulet' from UNDER THE NORTH STAR, and Faber & Faber Ltd and Harper Collins Publishers Inc. for 'Dog' from WHAT IS THE TRUTH?; D.H. Lawrence: to Viking Penguin, a division of Penguin Books USA Inc. for 'Self-Pity' from THE COMPLETE POEMS OF D.H. LAWRENCE. Copyright © 1964, 1971 by Angelo Ravagli and C.M. Weekley, Executors of the Estate of Frieda Lawrence Ravagli; Lois Lenski: to Mr Arthur F. Abelman of Moses & Singer (Attorneys), New York, for 'Sing a Song of People' from THE LIFE I LIVE. Copyright © 1965 by the Lois Lenski Covey Foundation; Myra Cohn Livingston: to Ms Marian Reiner on behalf of the author for 'Lazy Witch' from A SONG I SANG TO YOU. Copyright © 1984, 1969, 1967, 1965, 1959, 1958 by Myra Cohn Livingston; Roger McGough: to Peters Fraser and Dunlop Group for 'The Kleptomaniac' from PILLOW TALK (Viking, 1990); Eve Merriam: to Ms Marian Reiner on behalf of the author for 'Sing a Song of Subways' from THE INNER CITY MOTHER GOOSE (Simon & Schuster, 1969). Copyright © 1969, 1982 by Eve Merriam; A.A.Milne: to Octopus Publishing Group Library and E.P. Dutton, a division of Penguin Books USA Inc. for 'Happiness' from WHEN WE WERE VERY YOUNG (Methuen Children's Books, 1924); John Mole: to Peterloo Poets for 'Boo To A Goose' from BOO TO A GOOSE (Peterloo Poets, 1987). Copyright © John Mole, 1987; Edwin Morgan: to Carcanet Press Limited for 'The Computer's First Christmas Card' from COLLECTED POEMS; Ezra Pound: to Faber & Faber Ltd and New Directions Publishing Corporation for 'A Girl' from COLLECTED SHORTER POEMS; James Reeves: to The James Reeves Estate for 'W' from THE WANDERING MOON AND OTHER POEMS (Puffin Books); Carl Sandburg: to Harcourt Brace Jovanovich, Inc. for 'Metamorphosis' from HONEY AND SALT copyright © 1963 by Carl Sandburg and renewed 1991 by Margaret Sandburg, Helga Sandburg Crile, and Janet Sandburg, and 'The People, Yes' from THE PEOPLE, YES by Carl Sandburg, copyright © 1936 by Harcourt Brace Jovanovich, Inc. and renewed 1964 by Carl Sandburg, and 'Fog' from CHICAGO POEMS (1916) by Carl Sandburg, copyright © 1916 by Holt, Rinehart and Winston Inc, and renewed 1944 by Carl Sandburg; William Carlos Williams: to Carcanet Press Limited and New Directions Publishing Corporation for 'As the Cat' from COLLECTED POEMS; (published in the USA in COLLECTED POEMS, 1909 – 1939, Vol.1); Valerie Worth: to Farrar, Straus & Giroux Inc. for 'Sun' from ALL THE SMALL POEMS (1987). Copyright © 1972 by Valerie Worth.

Every effort has been made to contact all copyright holders. The Albion Press, in care of the publishers, will be glad to make good any errors or omissions brought to our attention in future editions.